👣 Chris Powling 👣

Illustrated by Philippe Dupasquier

🌳 ORCHARD BOOKS 🌳

For Len and the real George
CP

ORCHARD BOOKS
96 Leonard Street, London EC2A 4RH
Orchard Books Australia
14 Mars Road, Lane Cove, NSW 2066
First published in Great Britain in 1999
Text © Chris Powling 1999
Illustrations © Philippe Dupasquier 1999
The rights of Chris Powling to be identified as the author
and Philippe Dupasquier as the illustrator of this work
have been asserted by them in accordance with the
Copyright, Designs and Patents Act, 1988.
A CIP catalogue record for this book is available
from the British Library.
1 86039 824 3 (hardback)
1 86039 825 1 (paperback)
1 3 5 7 9 10 8 6 4 2 (hardback)
1 3 5 7 9 10 8 6 4 2 (paperback)
Printed in Great Britain

CONTENTS

Rosie fumbled in her pocket for a fifty-pence piece. Shyly, she held it out to Danny the Donkeyman. "Can I have a ride, please?" she asked.

"You?" said Danny.

He'd been watching Ben and Lola saddle up the donkeys they'd just unloaded from the van. Now he stared down at Rosie, frowning. "It doesn't apply to you, lass," he said.

Rosie bit her lip with disappointment. Then she saw the grin on Danny's face – a face so long and narrow he looked rather like a donkey himself. "I mean paying doesn't apply to you," he told her. "As from today, you're one of my helpers.

If it's a ride you want, be my guest."

"Right now?" Rosie gasped.

"The sooner the better, before the crowds arrive. Which of these splendid creatures catches your fancy?"

"That one," said Rosie, pointing.

"Ah," said Danny. "It's the big grey gelding you're after. Gorgeous George is his name. A beach-donkey, he is – or was before I bought him. Are you sure you don't prefer one of the others?"

"What's wrong with Gorgeous George?"

"Nothing, lass. Nothing at all. It's just that George is…George has…well, he's perfectly safe, I promise you. I wouldn't have him in the team otherwise. There's no denying he can be an awkward cuss, though. Mind you, he's incredibly popular."

"He would be," Rosie said. For George *was* gorgeous, no question.

Standing there, at the park gates, surrounded by Mary-Mary and Barney Rubble and Wideboy and Esmerelda and Her Ladyship – who were donkeys Rosie would soon recognise at a glance – George was the one who stood out.

For a start he was easily the tallest and his coat was a marvellous smoky colour – but it wasn't just that. Somehow, from the flick of his tail to the glint in his eye, he reminded Rosie of the sort of kid teachers keep right at the front of the class.

Ben helped her up in the saddle. Ben was as broad as a stable door and pretended Rosie was just as bulky.

"There are rules, you know, strict rules," he puffed. "How old did you say you were?"

"It's my birthday next week. But I'll only be nine, honestly."

"That's as maybe – but it's your weight that counts. A donkey's only allowed to carry fifty kilograms top whack, you know. That's about eight stone altogether."

"I'm much less than that," said Rosie eagerly. "Besides, George is big for a donkey, isn't he? That must make a difference."

"Quite right," Ben said. "He's almost thirteen hands high, George is – which is about as big as a donkey gets except for those Frenchified objects you sometimes see at horse fairs."

"Thirteen hands…according to the donkey books, that's measured up to here, the withers, isn't it?"

"Spot on, lass," said Danny approvingly.

Lola gave a loud sniff. "It needs more than books to know donkeys, Danny – especially a donkey like Gorgeous George." She was fixing the hay net to the hitching rail as she said this, taking care not to look at Rosie.

Rosie didn't like Lola one bit. She was too bony and brisk – not to mention her vinegary tongue. She was great with the donkeys, though, Rosie could see that. Where Ben was slow and rather clumsy and Danny himself had a bad back to cope with, Lola bustled about as if she were the real boss of the outfit. Already she was on her way to the van to fetch the wheelbarrow, the spade and the stiff broom they used to keep the pitch clean.

At last Ben finished checking the buckles. "All set then," he said. "Put your feet in the stirrups and don't let go of the saddle handle."

"Can I hold the reins?" Rosie asked.

"Sure you can – but there's no call to guide him, remember. He knows the way by now."

Rosie laughed at that.

As George moved off, Rosie saw the pitch stretching ahead of her like an old cobbled pavement. Alongside it was a slip road for coaches and beyond this a grassy bank where people could picnic. But Rosie's eyes were on George – especially on the dark markings of the cross which ran down his back and over his withers. All donkeys had one, she realised, but George's cross was clearer than most. "It's your holy bit, George," whispered Rosie, bending forward. "From the donkey that carried Jesus."

George's ears gave a short, sharp twitch.

Hastily, Rosie sat up. It was as if he'd just told her he couldn't care less about holy bits.

No, surely not…she was imagining things again. Her mum was always warning her about this. George was full of his own George-ness, that's all. There was nothing really unusual, was there, about his habit of tossing his head every now and then, more like a Derby winner than a donkey? "Calm down, Rosie," she told herself. "He's not Black Beauty, you know. Or Champion the Wonder Horse."

Even so, she was suddenly glad about the heavy iron railing, slotted through concrete posts, which turned the long, thin pitch into a sort of pen. By the time they'd reached the far end of it, she'd begun to relax again. Lifting the reins to the right, she pretended she was steering George into his turn – though she realised he'd have swung round anyway. Then, just as a test, she gave a gentle tug to pull him up.

To her surprise, he stopped at once.

Rosie couldn't believe her own skill. "That's brilliant, George!" she beamed. "I'm really riding you! Who says you're an awkward cuss?"

But she'd spoken much too soon.

Next morning, at breakfast, Rosie was still talking about George. "It was so embarrassing!" she exclaimed. "He just stood there not moving a muscle. I kept nudging him with my heels the way Danny and Ben showed me – but he wouldn't budge. Not a single step. In the end I was kicking him, practically."

"Poor donkey!" said Mum.

15

"Poor me," said Rosie indignantly. "I felt like a complete wally. Even Lola couldn't shift him and she's…she's…"

"Not your favourite person, I gather."

"No," Rosie sniffed. "She's not."

"So who finally got George going?"

Mum smiled as she asked this because she knew it was Rosie's favourite part of the story.

Rosie's eyes lit up. "It was me," she explained all over again. "I got down off his back, stroked his nose and just sort of whispered in his ear.

Eventually I must have said the right thing by accident, because he let me lead him back to the hay net ready for his first customer."

"As easy as that, then."

"Yes, it was. Goodness knows what was bothering him, Mum. Danny says it often happens. It's just Gorgeous George being his usual contrary self, he reckons."

"And you think there's more to it than that?"

Rosie nodded firmly. Her eyes were thoughtful now. Last night, before she'd gone to sleep, she'd looked through all Danny's books.

First, she'd turned to *Basic Donkey Health* then *Donkeys, their Care and Management.* After this came *The Professional Handbook of the Donkey.* None of them had been any help. Maybe Lola was right, after all, and it needed more than books to know a donkey. Or a donkey like Gorgeous George, anyway.

She heard her mother give a tactful cough.

Rosie knew what was coming. It was one of those moments when Mum felt she had to check up on things – on Rosie especially. "Mum," she said quickly, "I'm feeling better, I promise. I still miss the country like mad – and I can't really say I'm used to the city yet. But I don't mind moving here nearly as much as I did. Last night I didn't even dream about our old house."

"Didn't you?" Mum laughed. "What *did* you dream about, then?"

"Gorgeous George," said Rosie.

"Well, thank goodness for that! I was beginning to wonder if you were ever going to get over your homesickness, Rosie. What a stroke of luck that our next-door neighbour turned out to be Danny the Donkeyman!" Mum looked happier than she'd done in weeks.

Rosie felt a twinge of guilt about this. Strictly speaking, what she'd told her mother wasn't quite true. Last night she really had dreamt of Gorgeous George – but, in her dream, she'd still been riding him round and round the garden of the cottage they'd left in the spring. When Rosie thought of the flower-beds and the rockery and the apple trees she'd known all her life, and might never see again, she wanted to burst into tears.

Luckily, at just that moment, she heard a toot from Danny's van outside in the street. Rosie pushed back her chair at once. "He's ready to go, Mum!" she exclaimed.

"Have a good day, dear – and give my love to Gorgeous George."

By then, though, Danny's new helper was halfway down the front path.

Rosie stared and stared. "I just can't believe it," she said. "It's so...so country-ish!"

She was talking about the fields which spread out behind the garden centre. With the screen of trees all round her, she could hardly hear the traffic on the main road into the city. "There's so much room," she exclaimed.

"There has to be," said Danny. "I've got a dozen donkeys altogether – including a couple of young 'uns not four years old yet so they're not ready for riding. Also a couple of old 'uns past working age that I can't bear to part with. Donkeys need about an acre of land for every pair, lass. You can't coop 'em up like people."

"What about those huts over there?" Rosie asked. "They look like stables, Danny."

The donkeyman grinned at her. "Now that's a relief, I must say. Stables is exactly what they are!"

Rosie felt herself blush. Of course, she'd learnt from her reading that a donkey's coat isn't waterproof like a horse's. This means it must have a proper shelter when the weather is bad. She knew about the importance of keeping fresh water available, too – and of making sure that the fencing round their field is safe and strong. Donkeys are so clever, and so curious, they're the best escape artists in the world. None of this surprised her in the least. What was so strange, for Rosie, was seeing the pages in Danny's books come to life before her very eyes.

Also, she had to admit, being somewhere so country-ish still brought a lump to her throat.

Lola and Ben had already rounded up

today's team for the rides outside the park. It was the same as yesterday's. "And very trim they all look," Danny declared. "Well done, both of you. You've worked hard with the dandy brush this morning – know what that is, Rosie?"

"It's for grooming the donkey, isn't it? You start with the head and work your way towards the rear. The dandy brush gets rid of all the dirt and the sweat."

"Everywhere?" said Lola sharply.

"Not the tender parts, no. You use a sponge and cotton wool for those – after you've followed up the dandy brush with a body brush and a curry comb."

"Magic!" said Ben. "How's that for an answer, Lol?"

Lola's face looked bonier than ever. "Not bad," she snapped. "For someone who's never actually done it."

"Rosie will take her turn soon enough," Danny murmured. His voice was soft but none of them missed its firmness.

Especially Lola.

She scowled and turned away. Over her shoulder, she said, "They've all been hoof-picked as well, Danny. That's except for you-know-who. He's been playing up again."

"Gorgeous George?" Rosie asked.

"Who else?" Ben sighed. "He hates anyone touching his feet, always has. It's got to be done, though. He'll get cracks, otherwise – or seedy toe and suchlike. But he won't let Lol or me get near him this morning."

"Better be me, then," said Danny with a groan. "So much for my bad back."

"Or me," Rosie said.

"What?"

"Why not let me have a try?"

Before anyone could disagree, Rosie took a hoof-pick from Ben's grooming-box and walked towards Gorgeous George.

He was standing a little apart from the other donkeys. Or, perhaps, they were standing a little apart from him. You could tell at once who was Number One in this team. Rosie felt the eyes of everyone else – Lola especially – watching every move she made. She took a deep breath, and, a moment later, wondered what all the fuss was about.

Gorgeous George tipped up every hoof in turn almost before Rosie reached for it. Quickly and carefully, just the way the books had described, she cleared the mud and stones from each of them. Altogether, the job took no more than a couple of minutes.

Rosie could tell how well she'd done from Lola's reaction. "Quite the little expert, aren't we," she sneered. Then she turned away and bent over the water trough, her bony bottom sticking rudely in the air. That's when George bent down, too.

As he raised his head again, somehow his nose seemed to catch Lola under the seat of her pants and lifted her up, over and into the trough.

KERPLONK!

"Aaagh!"

It was hard to tell if the splash or the scream came first.

What's certain, either way, is that Lola was soaked to the skin.

"George, that was really naughty!" Rosie gasped.

"Better nip off home and get changed, Lol," Danny advised. "We'll see you at the pitch later on. Ben, look lively there – that trough needs filling up again. Lol seems to have emptied it all by herself."

"That beast's mad," spluttered Lola as she stomped soggily away. "He's completely bonkers, I swear it!"

He didn't seem bonkers to Rosie. If she were a donkey, she'd have done exactly the same thing herself.

More Misbehaviour

4

As the van turned on to the main road again, Rosie looked back at Danny's donkey farm. Already the sun was higher than the trees all round it, so that some of them were shadowy and some were green and golden. Also, she could hear the ding-ding-ding of a bell in a steeple close by.

The scene was so country-ish it hurt.

Ben and Danny didn't notice how upset she was. They were still talking about Gorgeous George. "He's a caution, that one," Danny said. "How long have we had him, Ben? Is it really only a couple of months? He's got into more scrapes in that time than the rest of the donkeys put together. Remember when he ate that American lady's straw hat? Tried to swallow it, he did, ribbon an' all, while she was filming the others with her camcorder!"

"Couldn't stand them being the centre of attention instead of himself, I expect," Ben laughed. "Like the day we hired him out for a wedding and he followed the bride right into the church. He knows he's a star, does our George."

"He knows he can get away with it, too," Danny nodded. "He's so big and so beautiful no one can resist him. If George decides to go walkabout that's when your troubles really begin."

"Walkabout?" said Rosie.

"Off on his travels," Danny explained. "Every so often he gets itchy hooves, does George. Wants to see if the grass is greener on the other side of the hill."

"So he runs away?"

"Given half a chance, he does. He can jump fences, trample hedges and even unlatch a gate if he has to. What's more, he's such a handsome devil everybody loves it when he drops in on them. They'd have anyone else arrested but all George gets is a pat on the back and a carrot."

"What about the donkey pitch?" Rosie asked. "Can he escape from that as well?"

"Aha!" Danny lifted a hand from the steering wheel and tapped his nose. "No way," he declared. "Custom-built that donkey pitch is. It was laid down by the Council nearly a hundred years ago.

My old grandpa was the donkeyman, then, and he made sure it was fit for donkeys in every particular. And that includes keeping tabs on a wayward beastie like Gorgeous George. Those stone pillars and that iron railing aren't just donkey-proof, lass. They're completely George-proof, too."

"I see," Rosie said. For some reason she felt sorry about this.

Or maybe, as the van shook and rattled on its way, she simply felt the city closing in on her again.

Not that she could see much of it from the donkey pitch. At one end was the flat, gusty, open heath. At the other, through a pair of impressive gates, was the Royal Park which stretched right down to the river. Danny pulled up in his usual place along the slip road. "Look sharp, everyone," he said as he switched off the engine. "There's no Lol to keep us on our toes this morning."

Of course, this made Rosie work harder than ever.

Soon, the donkeys were saddled up, the hay net and the water buckets were in place and the wheelbarrow, spade and broom stood ready nearby.

Rosie looked hopefully
at Gorgeous George. She heard
Danny chuckle. "Go on, lass," he said.
"You've earned your ride this morning,
I reckon."

In her head, as she pulled herself up in
the saddle, Rosie was shouting "Yippee!"

Maybe, somehow, George heard it. At
any rate, he broke into a trot straightaway.
Rosie's bottom thumped up and down on
his back as she struggled to find the right
rhythm. "What's the hurry, George?" she
called out.

They reached the end of the pitch in record time it seemed to her. Here, just short of the railing, George swung himself round so he was facing back towards the park.

Then he skidded to a halt.

Luckily, Rosie had been expecting this. She slumped forward on to his neck but didn't fall off, not quite. "George," she called, "George – whatever's the matter?" For the tall, smoky-grey donkey was trembling all over.

Was it the breeze, wafting up from the river, that he didn't like? Or the gulls, circling overhead, with their beady eyes and wicked-looking beaks? Maybe George just hated the noise they were making, because he suddenly threw back his head and began to bray: EE-AW! EE-AW! EE-AW!

It was the saddest sound Rosie had ever heard.

Danny wasn't at all impressed. "George," he said crossly, "this is getting beyond a joke. Rosie can handle it, I know, but suppose you'd behaved like that with a littlie up in the saddle? They'd have been injured more than likely – or scared right out of their skin. So just watch yourself!"

"Hey, Danny," shouted Ben from across the slip road. "There's a coach coming! It'll be here in a second with our first customers."

"Exactly," Danny said. "And they'll be looking for a ride that's nice, and safe, and normal. Any more nonsense from you, George, and you'll find yourself back at the Horse Fair with a price tag round your neck. Being a gorgeous donkey is one thing. Being a dangerous donkey is another."

And he turned away, rubbing his back.

Rosie stared down at her new friend in dismay. "George, he means it," she wailed. "If you keep on messing about like this, Danny may sell you to somebody else. Is that really what you want?"

Gorgeous George flicked his ears and didn't seem in the least bit bothered.

Rosie didn't believe him for a moment.

Twice more that afternoon George stopped in his tracks, tipped up his head and let out a bray so deafening it was as if he wanted to blast the seagulls out of the sky: EE-AW! EE-AW! EE-AW!

Rosie felt very ashamed as she gave the riders their money back – especially since Lola was watching her.

"Rosie," she snorted, "that creature's more trouble than he's worth. This morning he nearly drowned me and now he's losing us business. Put him back in the van. You can help with one of the other donkeys."

"Who says?" asked Danny, cocking his head.

"But Danny—" Lola broke off when she saw the look on the donkeyman's face.

Rosie heaved a sigh of relief. "You were lucky there, George," she whispered. "Maybe you won't be next time."

She could have sworn George answered with a shrug.

Later on, when the coaches were double-parked along the slip road, they had more customers than ever. "It's a madhouse," Ben grumbled. "We can't lift them in and out of the saddle fast enough."

"Better than standing around like a spare part, son," Danny remarked.

He'd winked at Rosie as he said this so he must have noticed how hard George was working. "Danny's forgiven you, I think," she told the big grey gelding. "Good boy!" "Good boy!" echoed the toddler on George's back. Happily, Rosie grinned up at him.

He was one of George's regulars – a four-year-old in a cowboy outfit who came to the pitch every day with his grandpa. He reckoned his name was the Texas Kid and Rosie let him pretend he was riding George over the prairie all by himself. "Good boy!" he kept saying. "Good boy!"

At the end of the donkey pitch, George swung round as good as gold. Also as good as gold, he began his walk back to the hay net. This time it was Rosie who pulled him up short. "Wait, George!" she cried out in alarm.

"Bus!" exclaimed the Texas Kid. "Big bus!"

It certainly was.

The coach looked as huge and sleek and gleaming as one of the cruise ships down on the river.

Already, as the driver tried to reverse, its massive back wheels had bumped up on to the kerb. Soon it was nudging the railing along the donkey pitch – bending it back and back – till, finally, it sprang loose from the concrete posts and collapsed on the cobblestones with a clang.

George spotted the gap at once.

Luckily, so did Rosie. Even as the donkey broke into a trot, she was scrambling up behind the Texas Kid. Gorgeous George went past the coach at a canter, picked up speed as he crossed the slip road and plunged into the picnic area. His hooves thudded round tablecloths, food and families – and no one seemed to mind very much. "Go donkey, go!" people shouted, waving their sandwiches.

"Yippee!" yelled the Texas Kid.

"George, where are you taking us?" Rosie howled, for he showed no sign at all of stopping.

He showed no sign of slowing down, either. With her arms locked firmly round the Kid and her fists gripping hard to the saddle handle, Rosie struggled to keep herself upright. "Just hold on!" she hissed in Tex's ear. "Whatever you do, hold on!"

"On! On! On!" came his squeals of delight. Encouragement was the last thing George needed. He took the road outside the park at a gallop, clattered along a stretch of pavement, then swerved smartly through a side entrance into the park itself. "Oh, no – not here!" Rosie gasped.

Ahead of them rolled acre after acre of fresh, green grass where tall trees cast long afternoon shadows. There were flower-beds as well, and a boating pond, and an orchestra playing on a bandstand. What damage would a set of flying hooves do to all this? Rosie shuddered at the thought. "Whoa-back, George, please!" she pleaded.

"Giddy-up, George!" squeaked the Texas Kid.

Rosie wanted to shut her eyes tight. She didn't though. She was too scared she might miss something.

Besides, nothing that bad seemed to be happening...well, not really that bad. The park keeper who fell into the rhododendron bush as George brushed past her might have overbalanced anyway.

As for the deckchairs in front of the bandstand, no one was actually hurt when George flattened them like a row of dominoes. Even sinking the canoe could have been a lot worse. The boating pond was only a metre or so deep, after all, otherwise he wouldn't have been able to wade across in the first place.

The two teenagers who'd been ducked were soon afloat again and paddling on their way. "They thought it was funny!" said Rosie in amazement. "And so did everyone else, pretty nearly."

This was true.

With every stride George took, the laughter and the cheering seemed to grow. Would George ever stop? A donkey can't gallop for nearly as long as a horse – Rosie knew that from reading Danny's books. Did George know it, though?

How long could Rosie, and the Texas Kid, hold on?

Welcome Home

Rosie needn't have worried. Outside the park, in a street running down to the waterfront, Gorgeous George began to lose speed. His gallop became a canter, the canter turned into a trot, the trot slowed to a walking pace.

The Texas Kid was furious. "Faster," he screeched, his heels drumming on George's flanks. "Go faster!"

"How can he?" Rosie protested. "Listen to his breathing, Tex. He's puffed out, poor thing. Besides, there are too many people blocking the road – can't you see that?"

Tex could – but he didn't have to like it.

All around them now were holiday visitors on their way to the Maritime Museum or to see the last of the great sailing ships in its special dock. Seeing George as well was an unexpected treat. "Hey, look at that donkey!" they smiled. "And look at those kids on his back!"

"He's big for a donkey, isn't he?"

"And such a wonderful colour – a sort of silvery grey. What a gorgeous animal!"

George gave his ears a little twitch as if he knew exactly who they were talking about.

What he also seemed to know was exactly where he was going. Rosie was quite sure about this.

"OK, George," Rosie murmured under her breath. "It's over to you now. Let's see what all this kerfuffle's been about."

George's ears twitched again. He took them past the museum and past the sailing ship, right to the edge of the quay. Here, he poked his nose through some fancy ironwork and peered longingly downwards. "What is it, George?" Rosie asked. "There's nothing over there except river – along with a bit of beach, maybe, because the tide's out. Have we come all this way for that?"

"Giddy-up!" said the Texas Kid hopefully.

"Hey!" Rosie yelped.

The Kid had got his wish. Gorgeous George was on the move again.

This time he didn't go fast, though, and he didn't go far – just further along the waterfront until he reached a set of ancient stone steps. "Down those?" Rosie said in amazement. "You're really taking us down those?"

Where did they lead, after all? Only to muddy-looking sand beside muddy-looking water.

The steps were steep as well. Carefully, George picked his way to the bottom like a sailor down a sloping deck. By now, the Texas Kid was beaming. He'd been to this kind of place before. "Seaside!" he declared. "It's the seaside!"

"No, it's not," said Rosie. But she could see what he meant.

Above them seagulls swooped and
hovered. And round them curved the bend
in the river. Here, small boats bib-bobbed
in the wake of bigger boats and long, low
barges lay at anchor.

Looking downstream, Rosie sniffed the air. Could that possibly be the salt-sea smell of the ocean? The Texas Kid seemed to think so. Already he'd slid out of the saddle. Using his hat as a bucket and his six-gun as a spade, he was hard at work on a cowboy castle.

So was George, apparently. He pawed at the sand where he was standing as if he really liked the chush-chush-chush of it under his hooves.

And suddenly Rosie understood.

Wasn't it obvious why the beautiful grey gelding had run away to a place like this?

Slowly, Rosie bent forward till her lips were almost touching the cross on George's neck and withers. "It reminds you of a beach, doesn't it," she whispered. "You've been missing the beach every minute since you got here back in the spring. I should have spotted that. Don't worry, George. Danny and Tex's grandpa will be on their way to pick us up, I'm sure...and I'll tell them everything as soon as they arrive."

She was certain they couldn't be angry once she'd explained.

And she was right. In fact, Tex's grandpa even gave her a ten-pound note for looking after his grandson so bravely. "Tex says it's the best donkey ride he's ever had!" he smiled. "Can he come back tomorrow for another one just like it?"

Later, as they drove the van back to the donkey pitch, Danny was still shaking his head in wonder. "Homesick, Rosie?" he said. "You reckon George has been homesick all along?"

"Well, he was a seaside donkey when you bought him, Danny. Isn't that true?"

"I can't argue with you there, lass. As it happens, he came from an old donkeyman down at Margate who was retiring. But he's a city donkey now. What on earth can we do about that?"

"Leave it to me, Danny. I'm an expert on homesickness. All he needs is a bit of patience, a bit of fun and a new friend to look after him. I'll sort out Gorgeous George for you, I promise."

Danny looked at her doubtfully. "Really, Rosie?" he asked. "You reckon you're up to it?"

"Oh, yes," Rosie answered.

"We're going to make a great team, George and me."

And she was right about this too.